THIS BOOK BELONGS TO:

. . . .

'018

?018

Other books by Emma Chichester Clark

I Love You, Blue Kangaroo!

Little Miss Muffet Counts To Ten

No More Kissing!

No More Teasing!

Up In Heaven

Will and Squill

Text © 1995 Laura Cecil. Illustrations © 1995 by Emma Chichester Clark.
This paperback edition first published in 2005 by Andersen Press Ltd. The rights of Laura Cecil and
Emma Chichester Clark to be identified as the author and illustrator of this work have been asserted by them
in accordance with the Copyright, Designs and Patents Act, 1988. First published in Great Britain in 1995 by
Jonathon Cape. Published in Australia by Random House Australia Pty., 20 Alfred Street, Milsons Point,
Sydney, NSW 2061. All rights reserved. Printed and bound in Singapore by Tien Wah Press.

10   9   8   7   6   5   4   3   2

British Library Cataloguing in Publication Data available.

ISBN 978 1 84270 491 2

This book has been printed on acid-free paper

PIPER

EMMA CHICHESTER CLARK

Andersen Press

To Laura

WHEN PIPER was a little puppy his mother used to say to him, "Always obey your master. Always look both ways when you cross the road. And always help anyone in danger."

ONCE PIPER was old enough to leave home Mr Jones, his new master, came to take him away. He was a strange, fierce looking man and Piper felt nervous.

"Don't worry," said Piper's mother comfortingly. "If you remember the three things I told you, you will be a good dog and I shall always be proud of you."

Mr Jones dragged Piper up a hill to the lonely
crooked house where he lived. "Tomorrow I want
you to take care of the rabbits in my vegetable patch.
Teach them a lesson they won't forget!" said Mr Jones
grimly. I can obey that command easily, thought Piper.

HE WORKED very hard. He took good care of the rabbits all day and by evening he had taught them to jump over him. They had a lovely time.

BUT MR JONES was furious. He came up behind Piper and hit him with a big stick. "You stupid disobedient dog!" he snarled. "You were meant to get rid of the rabbits! Stay in this hut until I decide what to do with you."

He tied poor Piper up, without any food.

BUT THE RABBITS didn't forget Piper. They visited him every night and brought him their food. Piper thought they were very kind, though he didn't enjoy eating lettuce.

A WEEK LATER Mr Jones
bought a new dog.

I T WAS A VICIOUS creature with teeth like knives.
"Brutus will get rid of all the rabbits," said Mr Jones.
"And then he will teach you how to be a real dog!"
Brutus growled at Piper and bared his sharp teeth.
Piper was terrified.

T HAT NIGHT Piper bit
through the rope and escaped.

He ran and ran through dark woods.

He ran up and down steep hills.

And he plunged across a river.

AT LAST he came to a great city. It was dark and
noisy. The houses were like grey boxes.
Everywhere cars and trucks hurried by. Piper looked
both ways and tried to cross the road. But the traffic
never stopped. He felt very small and alone.

THEN PIPER saw an old lady standing on the other side of the street. She called t him and he gave a friendly bark in return.

SUDDENLY SHE STEPPED out towards him into the road without looking! A car was about to run her over! Piper darted in front of her and stopped the car. But the old lady was so startled she fell backwards onto the pavement. She lay there without moving.

SOON A CROWD gathered and an ambulance arrived. The ambulance men gently lifted the old lady onto a stretcher and took her away.

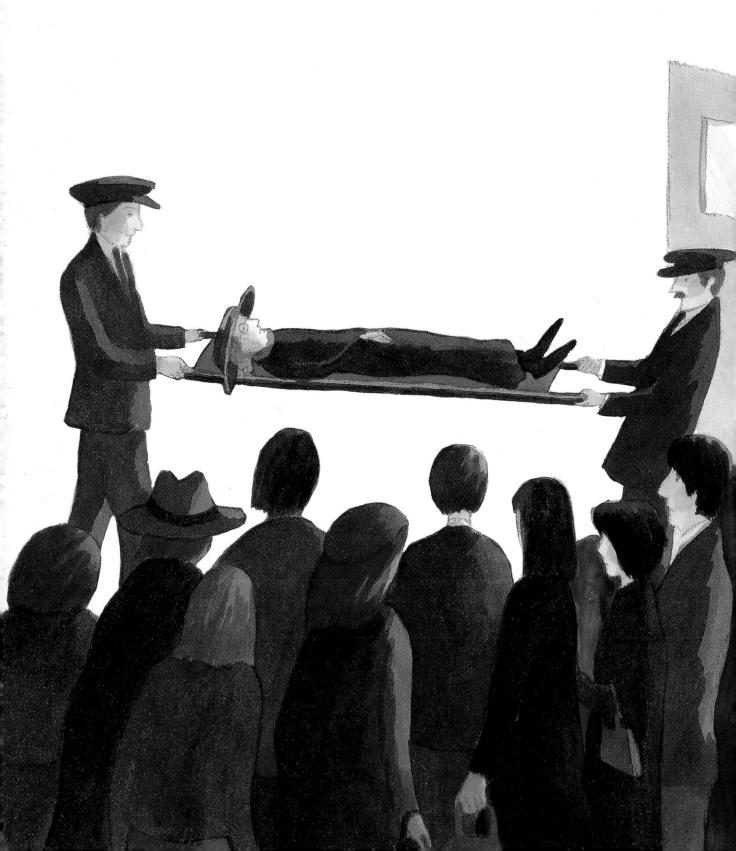

PIPER was miserable.
Nobody noticed
him sitting there, so he
crept away.

PIPER HAD BANGED his leg on the car when he saved the old lady. He limped sadly along until he came to a park.

IT BEGAN to rain. His leg hurt very much so he hid under a bush.

As HE DRIFTED off to sleep, Piper dimly heard voices through the raindrops drumming on the leaves.

S UDDENLY there was a loud shout nearby.
"I've found him!"

PIPER felt himself being gently lifted up and wrapped in a warm blanket. Then he fell asleep. He did not understand that everyone had been looking for the brave dog who had saved the old lady's life.

WHEN HE woke up he was lying on a soft sofa with a bowl of delicious food in front of him. And there was the old lady smiling at him! "You are a hero," she said.

"I'D LIKE you to live with me," said the old lady. "But I first I have to put up notices to say that I have found you, in case your owner wants you back. If no one claims you after a week then you can stay."

FOUND

Black dog, v. thin, long tail. Owner please ring 352794 within seven days if wanted.

PIPER couldn't explain that he never wanted to see his cruel owner again. Every day he waited in case Mr Jones called.

BY THE END of the week he was so tired he fell asleep beside the telephone.

Suddenly it rang!

T HE OLD LADY lifted the receiver and Piper heard Mr Jones's grating voice:

"That black dog is mine, but you're welcome to him. He is such a coward he won't even chase a rabbit!"

"I SHOULD hope not, you horrible man," said the old lady in a shocked voice, and she put the receiver down with a bang.

"How lucky I am to have found you," she said. "Now we can both look after each other."